THE BIGGEST EGG IN THE WORLD

To Mary
my Belfast
neighbour

[signature]

1991

Also by Marin Sorescu

Selected Poems 1965-1973 (Bloodaxe Books, 1983)
Let's Talk about the Weather (Forest Books, 1985)
The Thirst of the Salt Mountain (Forest Books, 1985)
[a trilogy of plays: *Jonah/The Verger/The Matrix*]
Dracula the Impaler (Forest Books, 1987)

MARIN SORESCU

The Biggest EGG in the World

BLOODAXE BOOKS

ISBN: 1 85224 021 0

First published 1987 by
Bloodaxe Books Ltd,
P.O. Box 1SN,
Newcastle upon Tyne NE99 1SN.

Bloodaxe Books Ltd acknowledges
the financial assistance of Northern Arts.

Typesetting by Bryan Williamson, Manchester.

Printed in Great Britain by
Tyneside Free Press Workshop Ltd, Newcastle upon Tyne.

Acknowledgements

This selection was made by Marin Sorescu from the following books:

15-31   *Norii/*Clouds (1975)
32-42   *Ceramică/*Ceramics (1979)
43-60   *La juventud de Don Quixote/*Don Quixote's Youth (1979), from *Tineretea lui Don Quijote* (1968)
61-62   *Astfel/*So (1973)
63-79   *Fîntîni în mare/*Fountains in the sea (1982)

Contents

Foreword

The Biggest Egg in the World is the second selection of Marin Sorescu's poems to be published by Bloodaxe Books. This new set of translations arose from different circumstances to those which shaped Michael Hamburger's pioneering work on *Selected Poems* (1983). Hamburger's selection covered the years 1965-1973, and he used German versions by Oskar Pastior as his channel of communication between the Romanian and English languages. *The Biggest Egg in the World* covers, for the most part, a later period – up to *Fountains in the Sea* (1982).

However, the book was conceived not only as a chronological follow-up, but as a tribute to Marin Sorescu by English and Irish poets who know him personally: David Constantine, D.J. Enright, Michael Hamburger, Seamus Heaney, Ted Hughes, Michael Longley and Paul Muldoon. William Scammell became involved at a later stage. Fundamental to the project was the presence of Joana Russell-Gebbett in Belfast. She is a Romanian friend of Sorescu's to whom he had been sending poems for translation into English.

All the poets except Michael Hamburger (who kept to his earlier practice) have based their readings on Joana Russell-Gebbett's translations. They may also have received some marginal signals from what Hamburger calls 'the recognition of Latin roots'. While the poets were choosing the poems with which they wished to engage, they often objected ruefully that it was hard to improve on Joana Russell-Gebbett's versions. Although scrupulously precise, these are very far from being prosaic cribs, and some have been included in their own right. So *The Biggest Egg in the World* celebrates translation – and poetry – as an act of collaboration. Like 'the phenomenal egg' itself, the poems have been 'passed from hand to hand...and gone round the world'.

On this journey they undergo various metamorphoses from the relatively literal recasting to the relatively free. Some translations function as sensitive interpretations, teasing out nuances. Some delight in Sorescu's great comic gift, others in the discovery of affinities between his imagination and the translator's. Thus criticism and creation also collaborate.

Among the affinities, it seems almost inevitable that Ted Hughes should have responded to the summons of 'The Whistle' and a supernatural bird ('Circuit'), as well as to the disintegrations of 'Warning' and 'Group'; Seamus Heaney to 'The First Word', 'Proper

Names' and the watery seductions of 'Fountains in the Sea'; Paul Muldoon to the enigmatic suggestiveness of 'Sentence' and 'Sweet Road'. In the latter, Muldoon conjures the rich internal rhyme 'camber'/'black-and-amber' out of the given scenario of a symbolic road with 'crushed bees'.

Patterns emerge if we follow all the translations by a particular poet – patterns which illuminate the poet as well as Sorescu. Of course the patterns are most pronounced where two poets have chosen the same poem. Thus Michael Longley's versions of 'Ceramics' and 'Map' emphasise the poems' mythic and archetypal dimensions; William Scammell's versions employ a slangier idiom which plays up the persona's self-mockery. Since no poet knew what another's hand was doing, it is especially remarkable how Muldoon and Heaney vary the angles on 'Oblique' or 'Angle' (page 64). They arrive at complementary phrasings of a haiku about art and society, which Joana Russell-Gebbett initially rendered as:

There pass across the sky, in fixed form,
The cranes,
The sonnets of the masses.

That translation seems to have sparked off two different fusions of formal and thematic possibility. Muldoon's 'passes'/'masses' rhyme imparts an epigrammatic finish and (in conjunction with 'rigid formation') an Eastern European political flavour. Heaney's assonance, 'lines'/'cranes'/'countrymen', harmonises a less ominous whole.

Most poets have adopted the freeish verse in which Joana Russell-Gebbett emulates Sorescu's procedures. At times, as in the above instances, they intensify his translatable aural strategies – refrain and repetition – by English metrical means. However, the fact that D.J. Enright and Ted Hughes find themselves formally at home suggests that Sorescu's poetry works by methods of structural dilation, which he sometimes abbreviates but no translator can foreshorten. He subtly dictates certain dynamics. And whether the poets stress his fancy, his irony, his symbolism or his myth, all perspectives and all rhythms converge on a unique combination of wit and weight.

Perhaps Sorescu's poems adapt so readily to translation by many hands because they are themselves a form of translation, even of Esperanto. He translates everyday phenomena, common experiences, into their emblematic contours: 'It is time to learn from the bats...' Always, as in 'Map', we follow the pointer. While Sorescu's parables are mysteries and riddles, they are also clarifications and answers. They have the universal accessibility with which fables override linguistic boundaries. The imagery, deceptively casual in its cosmic reach, maps a universe in which 'Destiny' gives human beings little room to manoeuvre – or to do anything except manoeuvre. The structure of the poems, too, both explores and imitates ironic collisions between free will and fate. Whether or not this reflects an unadmitted social and political context, Sorescu is raising large moral and metaphysical questions: 'Am I walking? Standing still?/ Still? Walking?' ('Detour'). His protagonists often end up in a cleft stick, trapped by logic and impossible desire:

> If only I could build myself a house
> As far away as possible from
> Myself.
>
> ('The House')

'Persecution Mania' sees no way out, even within the head:

> You steal away my days
> And I think you
> Are stealing away
> My days.

However, Sorescu's ungrateful Lazarus delivers a brilliantly calculated snub to the *deus ex machina*. And in 'Adam', man the fantasist, man the inventor, man the artist proves irrepressible:

> God had observed
> This disorderly creativity of Adam's.
> He summoned him, denounced him divinely,
> And expelled him from Paradise
> For surrealism.

'Disorderly creativity' – 'strumming' in David Constantine's version – gets the last laugh. Throughout *The Biggest Egg in the World* the resilient and resourceful artistic personality of Marin Sorescu powerfully unites all the guises it assumes.

EDNA LONGLEY
Belfast, April 1987

Destin

Găina pe care am cumpărat-o aseară,
Congelată,
Înviase,
Făcuse cel mai mare ou din lume,
Și i se decernase premiul Nobel.

Oul fenomenal
Trecea din mînă în mînă,
Dăduse ocolul pămîntului în cîteva săptămîni,
Și ocolul soarelui
În 365 de zile.

Găina primise nu știu cîtă valută forte,
Evaluată în băniți de grăunțe,
Pe care nu prididea să le mănînce,

Pentru că era chemată peste tot,
Ținea conferințe, acorda interviuri,
Era fotografiată.

De multe ori reporterii țineau neapărat
Să apar și eu în poză
Alături de ea.
Și astfel, după ce toată viața
Mi-o închinasem artei,
Am devenit deodată celebru
În calitate de crescător de păsări.

Destiny

The chicken I bought last night,
Frozen,
Returned to life,
Laid the biggest egg in the world,
And was awarded the Nobel Prize.

The phenomenal egg
Was passed from hand to hand,
In a few weeks had gone all round the earth,
And round the sun
In 365 days.

The hen received who knows how much hard currency,
Assessed in buckets of grain
Which she couldn't manage to eat

Because she was invited everywhere,
Gave lectures, granted interviews,
Was photographed.

Very often the reporters insisted
That I too should pose
Beside her.
And so, having served art
Throughout my life,
All of a sudden I've attained to fame
As a poultry breeder.

[DJE/JRG]

16

Destiny

The hen I'd bought the night before,
Frozen,
Had come to life,
Had laid the biggest egg in the world
And had been awarded the Nobel Prize.

The phenomenal egg
Was passed from hand to hand,
In a few weeks it had gone round the world,
And round the sun
In 365 days.

The hen had received who knows how much strong currency
Valued in pails of grain
Which she never managed to eat

Because she was invited everywhere,
Gave lectures, granted interviews,
Was photographed.

Often the reporters insisted
That I should be there too
In the photograph
Beside her.

And so, after having served Art
All my life

Suddenly I'm famous
As a poultry-breeder.

[TH/JRG]

I feel sorry

I feel sorry for the butterflies
When I turn off the light,
And for the bats
When I switch it on...
Can't I take a single step
Without offending someone?

So many odd things happen
That I want to hold
My head in my hands,
But an anchor thrown from the sky
Pulls them down...

It's not time yet
To tear up the sails.
Let things be.

[JRG]

Persecution mania

You wring out my strength
And I think you
Are wringing out my strength.

You carry my child off
To war,
And I think you
Are carrying my child off
To war.

You steal away my days
And I think you
Are stealing away
My days.

[DJE/JRG]

The shadoof

Sports at one end a bucket for raising water,
A boulder at the other end.
God dangles from my soul as heavily as that.
I'm pre-Big-Bang.
I'm the darkness he drags out miracles with.

Look, like a wheeze from my lungs
A comet's exploding into the void.
Keep out of its way, side-step –
If anything stops it in its tracks
That will be the death of me.

Mountains rise from my soul as well, horizons
Falling like fakirs on to fir-tree needles.
Sometimes a pore dilates to such an extent
A cloud-formation materialises
Or, better still, the salty sea.

I come in every shape and size.
I transmit myself for ever into the distance.
As a contrivance with a very long arm
I frighten the life out of death.

I crop up everywhere.
I'm all eyes and ears and I go on creating,
But I run out of universe like a well
At the end of a week.

|ML./JRG|

Looking for Hegel's portrait

I've never seen
Hegel's portrait,
It was momentarily missing
From all my books.

I've heard, though,
That in an antique shop
Not very far from here
There's a photograph of him. It shows him
Just at that period when he moves
Over every philosophical system
Like a silkworm
Over mulberry leaves.

It must be something unusual and beautiful,
Electrical,
Something like man.

One day I shall make time,
One day I shall hurry over there
And, asking all the words
To let me alone with Hegel,
I shall look at him silently
For several minutes.

[TH/JRG]

Precautions

I pulled on a suit of mail
made of pebbles
worn smooth by water.

I balanced a pair of glasses
on my neck
so as to keep an eye
on whatever
was coming behind me.

I gloved and greaved
my hands, my legs, my thoughts,
leaving no part of my person
exposed to touch
or other poisons.

Then I fashioned a breastplate
from the shell
of an eight-hundred-year-old
turtle.

And when everything was just so
I tenderly replied:
– I love you too.

[PM/JRG]

22

Warning

At night, as it happens, I forget about myself.
In the morning I have to recognise myself afresh
By my fingerprints,
By my tics especially –
I've got about a thousand specific tics.

If I look out of the window,
If I go to the office,
If I rock on my chair,
If I'm scruffy with ink on my fingertips

And especially
If I can't find my place anywhere
If I can't find my place
For ever and ever.

And if I'm put in difficult situations
(The straight walk, the staring at the moon).
It's strange that I don't recognise myself
Ever.

And each day
Have to get used to
Somebody else.

[TH/JRG]

The resurrection of Lazarus

What have you done to me, Lord,
Just when I'd managed to loosen up!

It was like having the mist lifted from my eyes
And I was beginning to see the darkness.
Now I realise the moon is different,
The joints of things are different too.

It was like having an opaque plug removed from my ears,
The true song had become clear to me.
You don't know what the secret sounds
Of a thought can mean, as it unfolds.

Now it feels as if someone has clubbed me on the head,
And I'm returning to my old bewilderment.
I hear that you are the one who hurt me so much
When you made the gravestone move aside.

[DJE/JRG]

The resurrection of Lazarus

God, what have you done to me,
Just when I was beginning to unwind!

It was like having my eyes demystified
And learning to see in the dark.
From a biochemical point of view
I was looking at a different moon.

It was like unmuffling my eardrums
And receiving the song of myself
Loud and clear on all wavelengths.
I made it up as I went along.

Now I feel I've been out for the count
And am coming round, punchdrunk as usual.
You are the burglar, the grave-robber.
You are the one who mugged me.

[ML/JRG]

The two thieves

The two thieves are important
As well.
One has stolen a candlestick,
The other has beaten an ox,
But they are very important as well.

This one in the middle,
What a big thief he is.
He has stolen so much glory from us.
If they hadn't talked such a lot about him
Perhaps some room would have been left for us,
We who are crucified askew.

[DJE/JRG]

The two thieves

The men either side, they are
Important too. One only stole
A candlestick, the other a cow but
Still both matter.

And what must he have stolen,
This one in the middle, the big fish,
Thief of our limelight,
Talk of the town? Without him
We should have had roomier deaths
Less crooked crucifixions.

[DC/JRG]

Heritage

From antiquity, from
The Middle Ages, from
All of history, anywhere,
Whole trainloads of errors
Addressed to us
Are still rolling in.

Tactical and strategical errors,
Political errors,
Gaffes of every sort,
Imbecilities, clangers,
Insignificant slips
Or drastic misjudgements.
On every track they're coming in,
By day and by night, round the clock,
So that pointsmen are suffering nervous breakdowns,

While we, the laughing heirs,
Only keep on unloading
And signing receipts for the stuff.

[MH]

Ulysses

The mere thought of what awaits me at home –
Those suitors, the swine, blind
Drunk, their greasy armour hung up,
Nothing inside their heads but the board game,
The dice as limp as their members,
Nothing doing, even if
A woman much more alluring than Penelope
Were ready for them. (Can she
Really be old by now?)

True, on the other hand, that tearful
Demented female at the spinning-wheel
Who gets all the threads in a tangle, out of sheer greed!
I can imagine the welcome at the gate:
– What on earth have you been up to?
– Troy wasn't child's play. So please let up.
– All right, but Agamemnon! Clytemnestra's
Agamemnon. How come he could be back so soon
That his bones are rotting by now?
Wasn't it everyone's war? –
– I was at sea for ten years, because Neptune…
– Leave Neptune out of it. Why don't you
Just tell me bluntly.
With whom?
And for such a long time?
What kind of sea could that have been? –

Huh, if only I could build myself
A hovel here on the waves,
Put up a tiny tent
Here on this rather more sheltered patch
Between Scylla and Charybdis.

[MH]

28

Ulysses

When I think what's waiting for me at home –
Those swine the suitors,
Blind drunk, their armour gathering dust on the pegs,
Playing backgammon all the time
Till dice and muscles waste away together
So they're no use for marrying,
Not even some old woman
Older even than Penelope
(Would she really be older herself?)

Not to mention that weeping woman
Who goes on spinning crazily, because of her nerves,
Witch that she is, tangling all the threads in the world!
I can see her at the gate, welcoming me:
– Where have you been?
– I've been fighting the Trojan War, don't nag…
– Well, well, but Clytemnestra's Agamemnon,
How come he got away earlier, he's already rotted by now,
Weren't you all fighting the same war?
– For ten years I wandered on the ocean, because Neptune…
– Leave Neptune out of it, please, and just tell me:
With whom?
And right up till now?
Really up till now?
Which ocean was it?

Oh if I could only make a little house
Here on the waves,
Raise a tent in this tiny corner
More sheltered
Between Scylla and Charybdis.

[DJE/JRG]

I'm like a stone

I'm like a stone
Lying on the ocean floor
Hoping to hear the echo of its fall.
Above me such a weight of water,
Great flood of water,
What can it do but
Fall to the bottom?

I'm terribly cross
When I catch myself
Waiting for
The echo.

[JRG]

Cure

When the cure for a disease is discovered
Those who have died of the illness
Ought to rise again
And go on living
All the rest of their days
Until they fall sick with another disease
Whose cure has not yet been discovered.

[DJE/JRG]

Ceramics

They have dug up
On the archaeological site of my body
A clay vase.

The vase is shaped like a heart.
An anonymous craftsman
Painted on it – long before Christ –
A sheaf of sunbeams.

Other folk have followed
And implicated their souls in the rays
With traditional motifs.

Now I add to the antique pot
Some up-to-date designs
So that the researchers of the year 4000
Will certify that I too existed
In the middle of the 20th century
Or thereabouts.

[ML/JRG]

Ceramics

Archaeologists have dug
into my body
and discovered a clay vase
shaped like a heart.

Some craftsmen who lived
before Christ decorated
it with sunbeams.

Other peoples took up
the theme, pointing their souls
with its rays and stars.

Now to this ancient pot
I add my bit,
the very latest in design,
so that the boffins
of the year 4000
will place me in the middle
of the 20th century,
more or less.

[WS/JRG]

Fresco

In hell, maximum use
Is made of the sinners.

With the help of tweezers,
Brooches and bracelets, hairpins and rings,
Linen and bedclothes
Are extracted from the heads of the women.
Who are subsequently thrown
Into boiling cauldrons
To keep an eye on the pitch,
And see that it doesn't boil over.

Then some of them
Are transformed into dinner pails
In which hot sins are carried to the domiciles
Of pensioned-off devils.

The men are employed
For the heaviest work,
Except for the hairiest of them,
Who are spun afresh
And made into mats.

[DJE/JRG]

34

Fresco

They end in Hell
Used up.

We pluck off with tweezers
Everything that served the women's looks:
Their brooches, rings and bracelets,
The pins that skewered their hair.
They lose their linen
We strip the sheets off the beds
They made and lay in and, boiling in pitch,
It is up to the women to see
The cauldrons don't boil over.

Some, if we choose,
Can be dinner-pails and visit thus
Our fat old devils
When they send out for a quart of hot sins.

The men likewise
We work them to a frazzle
All but the hairiest: those we set women unpicking
To make into doormats.

[DC/JRG]

Ballad

When lovers have caught fire all over
They hold hands
And together throw themselves
Into a wedding ring
With a little water in it.

It's an important fall in life
And they smile happily
And have their arms full of flowers
And they slide very tenderly
And they slide majestically on foot,
Calling out each other's name in the daytime
And hearing themselves at night.

After a while
Their day and night get mixed up
In a sort of thick sadness....

The wedding ring answers
From the other world.
Over there
Is a big beach
Covered with bones
Which embrace
And sleep in their exhausted whiteness,
Like beautiful shells
Which loved each other all their sea.

[TH/JRG]

Book-keeping

There comes a time
when we must draw
beneath ourselves a black line
and do the accounts.

Just when we were going to be happy,
just when we looked our very best,
just as we were going to overtop Erasmus
we met the fells, the oaks, the lakes
(are they still living? in what mode?)
whose multitudinous bright futures
we have already swallowed up.

A woman we loved
plus her failure to love us
makes zero.

A quarter-year of learned journals
makes a fodder of words
we ate in a week.

And, lastly, a fate
plus another fate
(hailing from God knows where)
makes two: we write one
and we keep one. Maybe,
who knows, there is an afterlife.

[WS/JRG]

Dreaming

Anywhere will do.
We've so much to tell
we fall down anywhere
and talk in our sleep.

Have we told the tables
and chairs, the locks,
the radiator, half
what we ought?

We talk to the dead
who, poor things, have
slipped back to God.

We talk and dream
until morning, when someone
puts on the light
and we start to talk
and all communication
is switched off.

[WS/JRG]

At the day-centre

The marks on the ceiling are brylcreem and
(I'm afraid) blood. Amazing really
Fifty years on the dole
And still leaping like fleas.
But as Churchill said
You can't keep a good man down. Admire
Their springy legs
And curious flat heads.

[DC/JRG]

Forwarded

There are days when the clouds
Appear to us like a flock of sheep,
Days when it frightens us to see a wolf
Merely depicted among the extinct beasts.

Our love comes back
So mountainous our hands
Feel over the tidy desk
For grass.

These memories come to us forwarded
From old addresses. They visit us home
With the loss of pasture.
We miss our flock.
We fear the wolf.

[DC/JRG]

Perseverance

I shall look at the grass
Till I obtain the degree
Of Doctor of Grass.

I shall look at the clouds
Till I become a Master
Of Clouds.

I shall walk beside the smoke
Till out of shame
The smoke returns to the flame
Of its beginning.

I shall walk beside all things
Till all things
Come to know me.

[DJE/JRG]

Solemnly

I carried my manuscripts
In armfuls
Into a big field,
I sowed them solemnly
And ploughed them under
In deep furrows.

Let's see what will grow
From these ideas,
From joy, grief, contentment
Crocuses or Christmas roses.

Now I am pacing up
And down the black field,
Hands behind my back,
More anxious every day.
I just can't believe
That not even one letter has sprouted!

One day for sure
This field will bloom with flames
And I shall stroll through them, solemnly,
Crowned like Nero.

[ML/JRG]

The whistle

Suddenly a whistle
Shrieks out
Behind a passer-by

Whose body fills instantly with sawdust
Like a tree when it feels
At the the edge of the forest
The saw.

Even so, says the man to himself, let's not look round –
Maybe it's for somebody else.
Anyway, let's have a respite
Of a few more steps.

The whistle shrieks
Piercing
Again and again
Behind every passer-by

They turn purple, yellow, green, red
And go on walking, stiffened,
Without turning their heads.
Maybe it's for somebody else –
Each one is thinking –
What have I done, only
One war, two wars?
And tomorrow I've the wedding
And the day after tomorrow my wife will give birth
In two days time I bury my parents –
I've so much to do, so many things.
It can't be for me.

A child
Bought himself a whistle
And went out to try it
On the boulevard

Blowing it impishly in people's ears.

[TH/JRG]

Angle

He placed a hand over his eye
And showed him the world,
Drawn large
On a board.

– What letter is this?
He asked him.
– The night, he answered.
– You're mistaken, it's the sun.
As we all know, the night
Hasn't any rays. And this one?
– The night.
– You make me laugh!
It's the sea. How could all that darkness
Get into the sea?
And this?
The man hesitated a moment,
Then replied:
– The night.
– Oh come, it's woman.
The night doesn't have breasts, my dear man.
Evidently you've been misled
By the dark hair. And this?
Take a good look at it
Before answering.
– The night again.
– Pity, you still haven't got it right.
This letter was precisely
You.

Next, please!

[DJE/JRG]

44

Balls and rings

My father the juggler
(called off on urgent business)
willed all his stuff to me.

Everything is rings and balls
he said. Remember this well.

The trees are green rings;
you must spin them round on your hand quickly, quickly
so not a leaf will fall.

The skies are blue rings;
a big push of the heart
and you twirl them round on your toes.
And women are another sort of ring;
they are wanderers, like the planets,
and you must describe epicycles
to save their appearance for the eye.

As for the balls, take care
not to lose the red one
or you'll ring down the curtain too soon...
Don't throw the black one
too far: our people
are.tied to it, under oath.

It's late, and father
shows no signs of coming back.
I've thrown up one more
than I think I'll be able to catch.

[WS/JRG]

Pond

The pond was a deep pond once,
The baits hung down
Like fruit, like shining fruit, lanterns,
Attainable planets and we
Went busily choosing a heart's delight
For the size of our mouths and rose flapping
Like angels. Now
Here we are in a crowd
In a muddy six inches gasping
For worms and the shadows
Of peering fishermen
Have quite put out the light.

[DC/JRG]

Sealess

Visibly, daily,
He was shrinking. The matter of him
Was taking its leave with polite excuses
Stepping back for the running jump
Into another mode.

And the sea too
The sea the poor codger was fishing in
The sea was pulling out.
Oh such an ebb!
One day he stranded on the mere sand.

She has gone with her waves and fishes·
Who knows where and moves now
To and fro, to and fro
Under some younger boat.

[DC/JRG]

The house

I want to build myself a house
As far away as possible
From all the things
I know.

As far away as possible from the mountains
Out of which squirrels leap in the morning
Like apostles in a clock
Naive beyond belief.

And I don't want it on the shore
Of that white tiredness
Where I could see through every window
An enamelled scale.

And I know all the tricks
Of the plain.
What else can you expect from her
If at night she frees the grass and wheat
To grow through your ribs and temples?

In any place at all
I'd get so fearfully bored
I couldn't even
Hang
On my wall
Pictures
The doorway would look too familiar
I'd be feeling I had to move on.

If only I could build myself a house
As far away as possible from
Myself.

[TH/JRG]

This earth

This earth reaches up to the sky,
The atmosphere, too, is earthy,
Earth atmosphere, that is;
In the roughs of gravity
Earth pours to earth as rain;
Icarus, Master Manole
Are of the earth, earthy,
And fall from roofs of earth
On to earth. Gravity is earth.

We live in earth.

Grow heavier in time;
Our foreheads sink
Deeper and deeper in earth.

Nor is there any death.
Since it's all the same where we are,
Now a bit closer to clouds,
Now a bit closer to oblivion
In earth.

[MH]

Map

Follow my pointer, please.
Three parts water, of course,
all to be seen in my bones and tissues.

Here are two poles,
the sea stars of my eyes.

My forehead, the driest part,
continues to form daily,
a wrinkling of the earth's crust...

And this volcanic island
if I am not mistaken
is my heart...I see
a road heading for my legs –
it must be my legs
or the road wouldn't make sense.

And all that blue stuff
flecked with white
is evidently my...er...soul
making its marble waves.

Note the long rivers
heading back towards tomorrow
and these rainforests,
the ineffable canopy of thought.

My five continental senses...
we take a double diurnal run
every day around the sun
and once round death...

That's more or less it,
my map of earth
which I shall spread out in front of you
just a little while longer.

[WS/JRG]

Map

First let me show you with the pointer
The three parts of water
That can be seen very clearly
In my bones and tissues:
The water is coloured blue.

Then the two eyes,
My sea stars.

The driest part,
The forehead,
Goes on carbon-copying
The wrinkles
Of the earth's crust.

This island of fire is the heart –
Inhabited, I seem to recall.
If I see a road
I think that's where
My legs should be,
Otherwise the road wouldn't make sense.

If I see the sea
I think that's where my soul should be,
Otherwise its marble
Would not make waves.

There are of course
A few other bright spots
On my body,
Such as my thoughts and experiences
Of tomorrow.

With the senses,
The five continents,
I describe two circles every day:
The merry-go-round around the sun
And the roundabout
Of death...

That, more or less, is the map of my world
Which will stay unrolled a little longer
In front of you.

[ML/JRG]

Going down

The moon is higher tonight
And no longer yours, the sky
Full of wonders has lifted off
Leaving you empty-handed.

Friend going down
If you are not ready for the basement yet
Reach for your boot-straps
Pack your living-room full of necessaries
Collapse it into the attic
And make for the mountain-tops
Rolling the slopes up after you. Get ready to pile
Ossa on Ossa on Ossa.

[DC/JRG]

Adam

Although he was in Paradise,
Adam walked the paths preoccupied and sad,
Not knowing what he was missing.

The God fashioned Eve
From one of Adam's ribs.
And the first man liked this miracle so much
That right away
He touched the adjacent rib,
Sensing a delicate tingling in his fingers
From firm breasts and sweet hips
Like the contours of music.
A new Eve had risen in front of him.
She had taken her little mirror out
And was painting her mouth.
'That's life!' sighed Adam,
And created another one.

And thus, whenever the official Eve
Turned her back,
Or went to the market for gold and incense and myrrh,
Adam brought an extra odalisque to life
From his intercostal harem.

God had observed
This disorderly creativity of Adam's.
He summoned him, denounced him divinely,
And expelled him from Paradise
For surrealism.

[DJE/JRG]

Adam

Adam in Paradise was still a sad man
Who walked with his head down
After something. Then God fleshed Eve
From one of Adam's ribs.

The miracle tickled Adam.
He wished hard and strummed a rung higher
And the curve of a girl, from the breast to the hip,
Pressed against his hand with a feeling music.

When she was separate
And he saw her tracing with her finger-tips
Her own smile Adam spent
Another Eve from his basket.

Eve Number One
God's promotion
Whenever she turned her back
Or was gone shopping for unnecessaries
Adam plucked at his cage
And a new Eve sprouted.

God got wise
And carpeted Adam. Son, he said,
Who told *you* to multiply?
Too much imagination, that's your trouble.
Off you go now, the hard earth awaits you.
Dig and delve.

(Exit Adam, strumming.)

[DC/JRG]

Playing Icarus

I went begging to the birds
And each of them gave me
A feather.

A high one from the vulture,
A red one from the bird of paradise,
A green one from the humming-bird,
A talking one from the parrot,
A shy one from the ostrich –
Oh, what wings I've made for myself!

I've attached them to my soul
And I've started to fly.
High flight of the vulture,
Red flight of the bird of paradise,
Green flight of the humming-bird,
Talking flight of the parrot,
Shy flight of the ostrich –
Oh, how I've flown!

[DJE/JRG]

Group

They'd been living together a long time
And were beginning to repeat each other:
He was her
And she was him,
She was her
And he was her as well,
She was, she wasn't,
And he was them,
Or something like that.

Especially in the morning,
Until they'd sorted out
Who was who,
From where to where,
Why this way and not that,
A lot of time elapsed,
Time poured away like water.

Occasionally they wanted to kiss each other
But realised, at some point,
That they were both her –
Easier just to repeat.

Then they'd start yawning with fear,
A yawn like soft wool,
Which could even be crocheted
This way:
One was yawning very carefully
The other was holding the ball.

[TH/JRG]

The compass

The sea is an enormous compass
With nervy fishes
Pointing all the time due north.

Each fish of course holds to
His own north
Which he tries to superimpose
On inferior norths,
Gulping them down while Neptune isn't looking.

Rumour has it that the time will come
For a unique north, scientifically worked out,
When all the fish
Will swim with the tide
Nose to tail
Formation-swimming northwards on their bellies,
Then southwards on their backs.

No longer will ships get lost
At sea
Or be sucked in by whirlpools,
And with such a high-tech compass
The world will, on the whole, have a clearer idea
Of where it stands from day to day.

[ML/JRG]

Hymn

Instead of roots the trees have
Saints,
Who have risen from the table
And knelt under the ground
To say their prayers.

Only their haloes
Have remained above –
These trees,
These flowers.

In turn we too shall be
Saints,
Praying that the earth
Shall remain for ever
Round and blessed.

[DJE/JRG]

The cave

There are rumours
Going about the cave:
About me calling you,
And you answering.

If our words haven't met each other
They'll go on looking for ever:
We don't know what the question was,
We don't know what the answer was.

We've launched our cries
Into the universe.
The words are watching each other,
They're chasing each other,
Mixing with the bats,
With the cracks in the stones, the holes in the water.
The howling goes on for ever,
Let's see what'll come of it
In the end.

[JRG]

London's tower

From London's tower
Heads fall
And sink
In coins that grow older and older.

Newton discovers
The law of gravity
And hits on a thought
Of mine.

[MH]

Hour-glass

Do I slowly empty
Or fill myself?

The same flow of sand,
Whichever way
You turn it.

[MH]

Fear or trembling

Standing by the window
I think of Saturn until
My thoughts
Arrive there
And Saturn begins
To use them
To think of me.

It's barb.
From the sky
Something stares at me.
Does that give me a fright
Or
Take fright at me?

[MH]

Socrates

How beautiful you look today
Sister hemlock,
Growing wild
Under my window.

In your supple waist
All the old wives' herbs
Triumph over nature.

And now you're even more
Cultivated.

[JRG]

Angle

Overhead, the traditional lines
Of cranes:
Sonnets for countrymen.

[SH/JRG]

Oblique

Across the sky there passes
a rigid formation of cranes –
the sonnets of the masses.

[PM/JRG]

64

The tear

I weep and weep a tear
Which will not fall
No matter how much I weep.

Its pang in me
Is like the birth of an icicle.

Colder and colder, the earth
Curves on my eyelid,
The northern ice-cap keeps rising.

O, my arctic eyelid.

[SH/JRG]

The teardrop

I keep trying to squeeze out a tear
that never quite falls,
no matter how hard I try.

It's as painful
as the birth of an icicle.

The earth freezes over
my eyelid,
the northern icecap gets bigger.

O, my Polar eyelid.

[PM/JRG]

Detour

I went round the world
Because it was in the way.

I told myself:
We'll have to go round
The world because it's
Blocking the way.

So it is, flip flop,
The sun's on your back,
Your heart's on a stick,
You hardly notice
The world is round.

To keep walking's
Another way of staying put.
Am I walking? Standing still?
Still? Walking?

[JRG]

When I want to take a rest

When I want to take a rest
I am ill.
Just imagine how ill
I shall be when
Dead.

[DJE/JRG]

The sentence

Each new passenger, on the tramcar,
is a carbon-copy of the one who occupied
the seat before him.

Either we're moving too fast
or the world's too small.

Everyone's neck is chafed
by the newspaper whoever's behind him's reading.
If I turned round right now
I'd be cutting
my own throat.

[PM/JRG]

Old people in the shade

You get tired quickly, you forget easily,
You start talking to yourself,
You move your lips
And come on yourself in the mirror moving your lips.

I have a fair notion of how old age will be for me.
For a day or two every summer, for a week
I am old.
Wrinkled, shrunk like a peach stone
In the kernel of the luscious day.

A Ulysses who keeps drifting off,
Forgetting where he's going back to,
Why he's astray on the sea,
Whether the war in Troy is over or coming.
A Ulysses unlikely to kiss smoke from the chimneys
Of home.

Are you straightening your tie there
Or strangling yourself?

40 degrees in the sun. I go into the house
And, with an ultimate effort of memory, remember
My name.
Torrid weather is much the same as old age.
The same sensations.

You trip on the rugs
You stumble over the slippers –
One of your nails has turned septic,
One of your teeth seems to be looser.

In the summer, we all come together.
We are all old,
Even the foetus in its mother's womb.

[SH/JRG]

Competition

One, two, three...
Here begins the hibernation contest.
All of you shut yourselves up in your holes,
And we shall see who hibernates the longest.

You know the rules of the competition:
You are not allowed to move,
You are not allowed to dream,
You are not allowed to think.
Anyone caught thinking
Is out of the game and no longer of interest.

You may only suck your paw
Like a pipe,
Which stimulates you to a profound understanding of
The phenomenon.

I am lucky to find myself next to a bear,
And when I get fed up with my own paw
I shall pass it on to him,
Taking his in exchange;
Which – as it happens – falls within the limits of
Permitted paws.

And though the Pharaoh Cheops
Has a start of several millennia,
I hope to overtake even him
With a formidable sprint,
Our celebrated sprint
In the sphere of hibernation.

[DJE/JRG]

The first words

The first words were polluted
Like river water in the morning
Flowing with the dirt
Of the blurbs and the front pages.
My only drink is meaning from the deep brain,
What the birds and grasses and stones drink.
Let everything flow
Up to the four elements,
Up to fire and air and water and earth.

[SH/JRG]

Proper names

When the ancient world foundered
Bottles had not been invented
So whatever was valuable there
Was rolled up
Into a few proper names
And set afloat on the water.

They have reached us safely, those names.

And when we uncork one,
Homer, say, or Pythagoras or Tacitus,
Great sheaves of light break open in the sky,
Millenial chaff falls on our shoulders.

Let us do all we can to increase
The store of proper names in the world
So that if the earth goes down
They will keep on floating,
Trojan horses with the whole of mankind in their bellies,
Headed for the gates of other planets.

[SH/JRG]

Proper names

When the Ancients set
They had pressed their virtue into proper names
As though into bottles
Which travelled well.

When we uncork, say, a Pythagoras,
A Homer, a Demosthenes,
The light spouts to the sky
And the good years fall about our shoulders.

Muck on the surface when *we* are scuppered.
Don't drink from us.
We blister the mouth.

[DC/JRG]

Evolution

It is time to learn from the bats
The between-creatures
Who can home in the dark.

Learn flying blind.
Dispense with the sun.
The future is dark.

[DC/JRG]

With only one life

Hold with both hands
The tray of every day
And pass in turn
Along this counter.

There is enough sun
For everybody.
There is enough sky,
And there is moon enough.

The earth gives off the smell
Of luck, of happiness, of glory,
Which tickles your nostrils
Temptingly.

So don't be miserly,
Live after your own heart.
The prices are derisory.

For instance, with only one life
You can acquire
The most beautiful woman,
Plus a biscuit.

[DJE/JRG]

Fountains in the sea

Water: no matter how much, there is still not enough.
Cunning life keeps asking for more and then a drop more.
Our ankles are weighted with lead, we delve under the wave.
We bend to our spades, we survive the force of the gusher.

Our bodies fountain with sweat in the deeps of the sea,
Our forehead aches and holds like a sunken prow.
We are out of breath, divining the heart of the geyser,
Constellations are bobbing like corks above on the swell.

Earth is a waterwheel, the buckets go up and go down,
But to keep the whole aqueous architecture standing its ground
We must make a ring with our bodies and dance out a round
On the dreamt eye of water, the dreamt eye of water, the dreamt eye
    of water.

Water: no matter how much, there is still not enough.
Come rain, come thunder, come deluged dams washed away,
Our thirst is unquenchable. A cloud in the water's a siren.
We become two shades, deliquescent, drowning in song.

My love, under the tall sky of hope
Our love and our love alone
Keeps dowsing for water.
Sinking the well of each other, digging together.
Each one the other's phantom limb in the sea.

[SH/JRG]

Sweet road

As though the light
were salving your wounds...

and the bees flying very low...

and the camber sweet
with their crushed black-and-amber.

[PM/JRG]

Seascape

Just when the sea seems as calm
as fresh tarmacadam,
the whales come out
to sprinkle it.

[PM/JRG]

Circuit

The top of the poplar in the garden
Is cast by the moon, through the lifted curtain,
Onto my bedroom wall.
The nest in the poplar is there as well,
Empty.

I dreamt of an extinct bird,
Strangely beautiful,
After which I was flying through the air
In the most natural way,
Flapping my arms.

I stopped in a poplar
To peer inside a house
Which even from the sky had caught my attention –
I don't know why.

Somebody was sleeping,
A tired man,
Deep in his sleep.

And on the wall above him
Stood the shadow of the poplar
With an empty nest.

[TH/JRG]

Let's talk about the weather

We've exhausted all the topics
So let's talk about the weather,
Everyone can say something
About the weather.

I, to open the discussion,
Shall say that it will rain
Because I dreamed a big cloud
Hung over my head,
And rained on me for ever,
Soaking my thoughts to the skin.

Let's have someone now
To contradict me, to speak for good weather:
For the next three centuries
The sky will be so clear
That we shall see one another
Without needing fireworks,
That's what he should say.

Someone else should talk about a dead leaf
Flying past the bare trees
Which no one can catch.
Tomorrow it will pass along our street,
Let's go out onto the balcony
And watch it too.

And that's how to hold this debate,
We'll argue with each other and talk so loud
The grasshoppers inside us will run off terrified.

The main thing is not to let silence come between us.
Everyone has to look happy.

[JRG]